My UNDEAD LIFE

TOTAL FREAK-OUT

by Emma T. Graves

illustrated by Binny Boo

raintree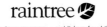

a Capstone company — publishers for children

Raintree is an imprint of Capstone Global Library Limited, a company
incorporated in England and Wales having its registered office at 264 Banbury
Road, Oxford, OX2 7DY – Registered company number: 6695582

www.raintree.co.uk
myorders@raintree.co.uk

Edited by Abby Huff
Designed by Brann Garvey
Originated by Capstone Global Library Ltd
Printed and bound in India

ISBN 978 1 4747 6190 1
22 21 20 19 18
10 9 8 7 6 5 4 3 2 1

British Library Cataloguing in Publication Data
A full catalogue record for this book is available from the
British Library.

WARNING! CAUTION! BEWARE!

This story has some seriously creepy stuff. Including:

- A very grumpy and hungry Tulah (me)
- Finding a job
- My first-ever middle school dance
- Runaway undead body parts
- Being completely, totally, horribly STRESSED
- Annoying little brothers
- Oh yeah, and <u>**ZOMBIES**</u>

Keep reading if you want, but don't say I didn't warn you.

6

7

CHAPTER 1

SLUUUUURRRRRP!

I sucked down the last drops of my embalming fluid and raw egg smoothie. Yes, it was every bit as delicious as it sounded. Then I put my cup down on my desk feeling . . . unsatisfied.

The formaldehyde mix had been whipped up by my friend Angela to keep me looking and feeling fresh. The smoothie would be deadly to the living, but it was a real after-lifesaver for this zombie. The special embalming chemicals in it stopped corpses from going bad. It was pretty much the only thing keeping me from turning into a pile of rotting dead meat.

Angela had also added a few eggs to the recipe. They were supposed to help control my hunger and the bad moods that came with it. But lately it hadn't been doing the trick.

I looked at the empty cup and sighed. After downing my whole Sunday supply of smoothies, I was still starving.

To distract my hollow stomach, I turned back to the sewing tutorial I was watching on my laptop. I'd been trying to dedicate my weekends to learning useful zombie hacks.

You'd be amazed how handy sewing was to the undead. See, when you were no longer living, you tended to lose parts. Not long ago, I had to reattach my pinky on opening night of the school musical. (Thank goodness we found the finger in my dress pocket and not rolling around onstage!)

Ever since then, I'd been trying to improve my stitching skills. Angela was there to help that night of the musical, but what if I lost a toe when I was by myself? Or worse?

I tried to make a knot in the thread so I could practise a stitch. It wasn't easy when you couldn't feel your fingertips very well.

GRRRRRRRRRRR!

Without thinking I let out a growl as the thread slipped out of my fingers. I felt like kicking my desk, turning it over and smashing it to bits – only I'd probably do more damage to myself.

I took a big breath and tried to keep my cool. Not only was I feeling more and more hungry lately, but being hungry was making me more and more grumpy.

Deep breaths weren't going to solve this problem. I needed food. NOW!

I yanked open my bedroom door and grumbled my way to the kitchen.

My little brother, Jaybee, was already there. He was leaning into the refrigerator. Luckily, my parents were in the back garden. They liked to garden together at the weekends.

I charged towards the fridge. "Out of my way!" I shouted, shoving Jaybee across the kitchen.

"Ow! Tulah!" he yelled as he ran into the worktop.

Jaybee held his side and rubbed the sore spot, but I didn't care. I needed meat! Raw meat!

I checked my options in the fridge. I'd used the last egg in my smoothie. Everything else – all the food that I had loved back when I was a living vegetarian – looked disgusting!

Cheese? Hard block of yuck.

Peanut butter? Slimy brown slop.

Hummus? Beige blech.

Baby carrots? Orange vomit nuggets.

I didn't even like cereal anymore! It was almost unbelievable. I mean, who didn't love sugary, crispy flakes?

Me.

"*UUUUUGGGGGGGHHHHH,*" I groaned.

All normal foods made me ill. Like, they actually repulsed me. Even if I managed to choke something normal down, it came right back up. And it wasn't pretty. The ONLY thing I could eat (and the only thing I craved) was raw protein. That meant a diet of raw chicken, raw beef and raw eggs.

I slammed the fridge closed and pulled open the freezer.

"Are you OK?" Jaybee asked. He still stood back near the worktop. He hadn't taken one step closer to me.

I whirled on him. "What do you think?" I snarled. "Do I look *OK?*"

Jaybee stayed quiet.

I think I scared him.

I think I scared myself!

You must get food before you lose it! I told myself.

I discovered a frosty package of chicken buried under some peas. I grabbed it from the freezer and tore it open.

I gnawed hungrily on it. The meat was as hard as a rock, so I had to be careful not to loosen (another) tooth. But if I waited for the chicken leg to thaw, I might end up chewing off my brother's leg instead!

NO! I quickly banished that image from my head. That was a long, dark road I could never, EVER go down.

I might be a zombie, but I would not become a cannibal. I was civilized. Eating like a civilized zombie was still, shall we say . . . a challenge. Especially keeping my new food preferences from my parents.

So far I'd been doing OK, thanks to Jaybee's help. (Yet another reason not to chew off his leg.) My brother had been working hard eating enough normal food for the both of us. It was a good thing he was going through a growth spurt!

I had also told Mum and Dad that I was on a protein diet. Then I secretly chowed down on all the raw meat I could get my stiff fingers on.

I whipped the door shut to the nearly-empty freezer. But as the pickings grew slimmer, I got more and more testy. I had to admit that I had a serious "hanger management" issue.

Because hunger + anger = HANGER. And one very unhappy zombie.

Jaybee edged closer. "Tulah? We've got to do something about you. I mean, this." He waved his hand toward the frozen wasteland that was the freezer. "Your hunger temper tantrums are off the charts. You're going to be dead for the rest of your life. You need to work out how to get food."

"I know," I moaned as I finished chewing my frozen chicken. "But what can I do?

If I ask Mum and Dad to buy more meat, they're going to start suspecting something is up."

I couldn't bear the thought of my parents looking at me like the monster I was. "They can't find out!" I shouted.

I slammed my hand down onto the kitchen table. Something went flying. Jaybee dodged to the right to avoid getting hit by the tiny object.

I gasped and quickly counted my fingers – they were all there. I let out a big breath. I'd only lost my grip on the chicken bone. And I'd lost control of my temper . . . again.

Jaybee shook his head as he picked up the bone and put it in the bin. Then he silently started smearing pieces of bread with peanut butter and jam. It was easy for *him* to get a snack whenever he wanted.

I tore into the other chicken leg. I started to feel a little better, and then a little worse. Jaybee was still watching me out of the corner of his eye. It was like he didn't trust me. Like he was ready to run at any second.

Now that my hunger was letting up, I really saw how out of control I was. I mean, my little brother was afraid of me!

"Sorry, Jaybee," I apologized. "I didn't mean to bite your head off."

Jaybee dropped his knife. "What? You were going to bite my head off?" He looked at me wide-eyed.

"No! No!" I said, holding up my hands. "It's an expression. I just meant that I'm sorry I snapped at you."

"No biting!" Jaybee said, pointing at me. "Don't even joke about it."

"I promise!" I said.

"We've *really* got to do something about this . . . ," Jaybee repeated, backing out of the kitchen with his sandwich. "And by *we*, I mean *you*."

I was alone. I slumped down into a chair at the dining table. I was going to have to solve this problem by myself. I could hardly blame Jaybee for not wanting to be involved. He'd already been a huge help with my other undead issues, but at this point I might be asking him to risk his life.

As a zombie film and comic buff, Jaybee did not take the threat of a bite lightly. He might be OK with helping a zombie, but he was not eager to become one.

While my head cleared, I took the chicken packaging to the outside bin. I peeked into the back garden, where my parents were still busy planting and raking. I didn't want them to see suspicious meat waste in the bin under the sink. I didn't want our dog, King Kong, to drag it out either.

I lifted the lid to the big rubbish bin next to the house. But before throwing away the evidence of my meat-eating, I stared down at the wrapper. The price sticker stared back at me. *That* was the real problem.

Eggs were a good source of cheap, raw protein, but they weren't cutting it anymore. I needed more meat, and meat cost money.

I couldn't ask my parents for extra cash without them getting suspicious. I'd already used all my own savings. I had spent it all on buying minty gum and deodorant spray to cover up my death breath and dead body odour. (That was before Angela came up with the embalming smoothie solution to stop me from rotting.)

So there was only one thing for me to do. I had to find a job, and soon.

CHAPTER 2

"Don't you get pocket money?" Angela asked.

I had confessed my problem to my two besties, Angela and Nikki, on Monday at lunch. I was so anxious to tell them about my latest problem that I had even followed them into the cafeteria – a place I tried to avoid after the Mystery Meal disaster.

I'd spent the whole night before trying to come up with a solution. I couldn't think of anything. (Talk about feeling brain-dead!) Seriously, I no longer required sleep and had plenty of time to brainstorm. You'd think I might have come up with *something*. But I had zero ideas.

I was officially desperate and hoping three heads would be better than one.

"My pocket money would barely cover a chicken foot," I told my friends, eyeing the strap on Angela's backpack. It looked like it might be leather. It also looked like it might be tasty. "Meat is expensive. So this job has to be good."

"Well, what do other twelve-year-olds do for money?" Nikki wondered out loud.

"There's pet-sitting," Angela said, moving her delicious-looking bag to the floor. "I watched my cousin's pet snake, Noodle, once. I made thirty bucks."

"Or there's babysitting," Nikki added. She started unpacking her lunch onto a napkin.

Nikki and Angela never ate school food anymore. It was hard to trust the cafeteria when one meal had turned your friend into a member of the living dead. Today Nikki had a turkey sandwich, carrot sticks and yoghurt. YUCK!

"You babysit sometimes, right?" Nikki
asked.

"Yeah, but pet and babysitting are only
now-and-then jobs, when people go out,"
I said. "I need a regular job so I can get
steady cash, so I can get a steady supply
of food. That's the whole *problem*!"

I dropped my head to the table, feeling
hopeless and hungry. The eggless smoothie
I'd downed for breakfast hadn't even put
a dent in my cravings. I was starved. And
pretty grumpy too.

"What about a paper route?" Angela
suggested as she unwrapped her lunch. It
looked just as horrible as Nikki's. "You don't
sleep anymore, so you'd already be up in
the early morning anyway."

"That's not a bad idea," I admitted.
But then I sighed. "Except hardly anyone
in my neighbourhood gets the actual paper
delivered. Everyone just reads the news on
their phones."

My eyes kept darting around the cafeteria. It was almost like I was expecting to see a steak walk by at any moment. If I did, I would tackle it.

"What about something else where you can get a *graveyard* shift?" Nikki suggested, waggling her eyebrows.

"I need you to get real, Nikki!" I snapped. "Who's going to hire a kid to work during the night? I'm sure there are a few laws against that."

"Calm down, Tulah. It was just a joke. Get it, *graveyard?*" Nikki asked. She shook her head. "You're losing your sense of humour."

"Sorry, I didn't mean to be so harsh," I said. I hugged my stomach. "I'm just too hungry to enjoy puns right now."

My mood was getting worse by the minute. The three of us were still sitting there, straining our brains, when a familiar voice made me jump.

"What's going on over here?" the voice said. "You guys look like somebody died."

I turned around to see my crush, Jeremy Romero, and his two best friends, Noah and Charlie. They were standing right behind me and holding their hot lunch trays. OMG.

"N-n-nobody died!" I said, probably a little too forcefully.

I hoped I didn't look as freaked out as I felt. I wondered how long the guys had been standing there, and how much Jeremy might have heard.

I glanced around at our table and faked a smile. Everything looked normal, right?

Wrong! I realized that I was the only one without a lunch. Definitely not normal.

I grabbed half of Nikki's sandwich and shoved it into my mouth.

Jeremy gave me an odd look. "Seriously, is everything OK?" he asked. "You guys seem a little gloomy."

Jeremy flopped into the seat opposite me and put his tray down. Noah and Charlie found spaces too.

Angela stared at Jeremy while I chewed and chewed Nikki's sandwich. Angela was used to being called gloomy, or goth, or emo. Her family owned the only funeral home in town (which is how she got the embalming fluids for my smoothies), and she always wore black.

"We're totally fine!" Nikki chirped.

I wished that were true. I kept chewing, but I was *not* fine. Nikki's sandwich tasted worse than dirt. It felt like a glob of wriggling worms in my mouth. I wasn't sure how I was going to swallow.

I pressed my lips tightly together to hold in the bite. *Just act normal,* I told myself.

But it wasn't easy keeping my cool. Not here in the awful cafeteria. Not with a ball of blech in my mouth, and definitely not in front of dreamy Jeremy Romero.

I'd had it bad for Jeremy ever since he started at Evansville Middle School this past year. My crush and I had shared the stage in *Musical High*, plus a few stage kisses too. It had been great – maybe even better than great.

Without the rehearsals and shows to get us together, we didn't see each other much anymore. We hadn't really talked.

Until now. Jeremy was here. He was sitting across from me. He was waiting for me to say something. But all I could do was chomp on the nasty wad of glop in my mouth.

I finally managed to gag down the disgusting, over-chewed bite of sandwich. "So, what's up?" I croaked.

"Yeah, Jeremy. *What's up?*" Noah said. I could tell he was teasing him.

Jeremy cleared his throat. Nikki and I exchanged a look.

"Didn't you have something you wanted to ask Tulah? About the *dance*?" Charlie added.

OMG, the dance! I'd been so worried about my meat problem I'd forgotten that our first-ever middle school dance was happening a week from Friday.

Is Jeremy going to ask me to the dance right now, in front of everybody? I wondered. It'd be a dream come true!

I was fighting back a grin when all of a sudden I had to fight back something else. But I lost the battle.

A huge burp erupted out of me. Everyone turned to stare.

I gave a tight smile. I wanted to open my mouth to excuse myself, but the bite of sandwich I'd forced down was really moving now. It was swirling and growing in my stomach. It felt like the ever-expanding alien monster in one of Jaybee's favourite films, *The Blob.*

And The Blob wanted out.

28

"How are you doing in there?" Nikki asked from outside the toilet cubicle.

She and Angela had followed right behind me. Hopefully they didn't arrive in time to hear The Blob hitting the toilet bowl water. Gross!

I leaned back from the toilet. "I'm fine," I said, closing my eyes for a second.

As soon as the normal food was gone, all I felt was embarrassed. I couldn't believe what had just happened. I'd almost puked on the guy I liked and . . .

"Wait," I said, "did Jeremy Romero really ask me to the dance . . . *committee*?"

"Uh-huh," Nikki replied.

"*Ugh*. That's what I thought," I grumbled. I stood up from the floor and stumbled towards the sinks. I washed my hands in cold water twice to let the news sink in.

"I mean, I thought he was going to ask me to the actual dance," I said.

"That's what I thought too," Nikki said. "But hey, the dance committee is better than nothing, right? At least Jeremy will be there."

"I guess, but I don't know if I have time to join any party planning groups," I argued. "What about my food issue, and finding a job, and—"

"I think it'd be good for you," Angela interrupted. She always got straight to the point. "You need to stop worrying so much. You stressed about the musical, but that turned out fine."

I crossed my arms. "Well, would you guys join too?" I asked.

"Of course!" Nikki said immediately.

Angela wrinkled up her nose.

"It'll be fun!" Nikki insisted. She nudged Angela, and our favourite goth girl gave a grudging nod. Dances were not exactly Angela's scene, though she had been branching out lately.

"Then it's decided," I said. I clutched my empty stomach. "Just, please, remind me to *not* eat any of the snacks."

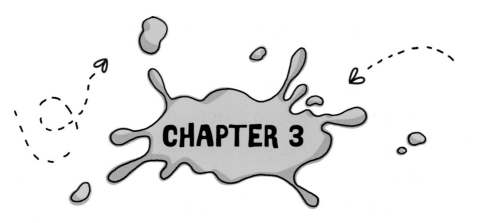

CHAPTER 3

The first thing I did when I got home was drop my bag and head for the kitchen. I was so desperate to find some food that I almost tripped over our dog, King Kong, when he rushed to greet me.

"Look out!" I shouted as I lurched past him.

After losing my lunch (well, Nikki's lunch) at school, I was hungrier than ever. It had taken every bit of self-control not to eat Ms Rogi's goldfish during our biology lesson at the end of the day.

My mood wasn't any better either. I'd nearly screamed at someone who had bumped into me on my way to the bus.

I yanked open the refrigerator door and scanned the shelves, hoping for a miracle. King Kong stood panting beside me. I guess he was hoping for a miracle too.

We were both disappointed. The shelves were still as bare as they had been that morning. No meat. No eggs. Nothing good for a growing zombie or a begging dog.

"Just great," I muttered.

It used to be when the fridge was this empty I would get excited. It meant we would probably have takeaway for dinner. I used to love takeaway. But my food needs had changed. What kind of restaurant delivers heaps of raw meat?

I opened the freezer, even though I knew I would find more of the same. Nothing.

"*Arrrgh!*" I groaned.

"Woof!" King barked back at me.

I looked down at the cute little French bulldog. He was wagging his tail and licking his lips, hoping for some extra nibbles.

"Sorry, King," I said. "You're only getting your normal supper."

That made me think.

"Dog food?" I wondered out loud.

Why not? At this point I was willing to try anything. Wet dog food didn't *look* cooked.

I got a can from the cupboard. I peeled back the lid and took a taste.

"*Blech!*" I coughed.

I'd hoped the dog food would be all raw protein, or at least have enough in it to calm my fierce appetite. But no. This slop was definitely cooked and definitely disgusting!

"It's all yours, buddy," I said.

I let the whole mess slide out of the can and into King's bowl. At least one of us could eat.

As I watched King wolf down the brown mess, I stifled another groan. Why was eating so easy for everyone but me?

When he had finished his bonus meal, King wandered off. He soon found one of his old bones under the dining table and began to chew. And chew. And chew.

CRRUNK CRRUNK CRUUNK

His teeth scraped against the hard bone. I slumped over the worktop and watched. I hate to admit it, but that sound made me jealous. I wanted that bone!

I lumbered over to the table and kneeled down. "Hey, King. Can I borrow that?"

I reached a hand towards the bone. King Kong bared his teeth. I bared my teeth. King growled.

"Fine. I hear you," I mumbled, standing back up.

He was telling me to get my own food, and he was right. I was being ridiculous.

I was suddenly very glad Jaybee had football practice after school today. I didn't want him to see me acting like such a weirdo.

I stumbled into the living room to look for spare coins. *Maybe I can round up enough to buy a packet of chicken wings,* I thought.

Except I knew the chances of me finding extra money lying around. It was exactly the same as a zombie food van pulling up to hand out free meat – absolutely zero.

As I searched underneath the sofa cushions, my phone buzzed. It was a text from our neighbour.

MRS GREGOR*: Hi, Tulah! Sorry for the short notice, but are you available to watch the kids and feed them dinner? Stewart is away and I need to go and help my sister.*

I pumped my fist. Bingo!

I immediately started typing my reply. The Gregors lived next door. Their kids, Libby and Max, were four and six. I'd babysat for them before.

But that was, you know, *before*.

My thumbs stopped. I stared at my phone. Honestly, in my current state, babysitting could be risky. A responsible babysitter would never want kids to be watched by the undead – and definitely not the very, very hungry and grumpy undead.

I heard King's teeth scrape on his bone again, and every thought but one flew right out of my head. *Money equals meat.*

I hit SEND.

ME: *I'll be right over!*

I quickly scrawled a note for Jaybee. He would be home from football soon. Then I shot a text to my parents to let them know I was going next door. Three minutes later I was standing on the Gregors' doorstep.

"Tulah! Tulah!" Libby and Max started chanting my name and jumping up and down as soon as they spotted me. The quick change of plan must've got them hyped up. Plus they liked me. Or at least the old me, anyway.

I lurched through the door and listened to Mrs Gregor's rundown about emergency numbers and other important info for the night. All the while I tried to look happy, responsible and super alive.

"There are hot dogs and green beans for dinner," Mrs Gregor finished. "Thanks again, Tulah!"

I tried not to let her see me scowl as Max and Libby hugged her goodbye. Hot dogs were meat (in theory), but they were already cooked. The small hope I'd had of being offered something raw and bloody for dinner disappeared. Of course, there was still the freezer to check.

Mrs Gregor gave a final wave and then went out the door. I turned towards the kids.

"So, do you guys want to play a game?" I asked.

Max and Libby shrieked and ran to the living room where they had a huge stash of games. If I could get them started on one, I'd be free to raid the freezer.

"Twister! Twister!" Libby shouted as I started sorting through the boxes.

"How about Go Fish?" I said.

"No! Twister!" Libby insisted.

"Draughts?" I asked.

"Twister!" Libby shouted again.

My plan failed, miserably. I took the game out of the cabinet. "Fine," I snapped. Then I immediately felt bad. So I added more gently, "Can I spin?"

"No, Tulah. You play! I spin da spinner!" Libby yelled while Max spread out the plastic play mat.

I sighed and handed the spinner to Libby. It was no use arguing with a four-year-old. I stood on one side of the mat. So much for sneaking back to the kitchen.

"This hand red!" Libby called, holding up her left. Max and I obeyed.

"Tulah, your arm!" Libby yelled. "It looks broken!"

"And your leg!" Max added, looking up from the mat. "What's wrong with it?"

I immediately stood up. "You win, Max!" I announced. "Don't worry about me. Nothing's broken."

I popped my shoulder back in as quickly as I could. Then I fixed my leg. I smiled widely at the kids. They stared at me like I was a freak. Because I *was* a freak.

"See? I'm just double-jointed!" I said, trying to sound cheerful. "Everywhere."

Libby and Max smiled back nervously, but I wasn't sure they were convinced.

"How about I go and start dinner?" I asked and backed out of the living room. Nobody argued.

As I made my exit, I almost tripped on a white and orange furball. It was Bugle, the Gregors' cat (and King Kong's nemesis).

"*Mrow*," Bugle said, winding all around my legs.

Mrs Gregor hadn't said anything about feeding the cat, but Bugle followed me into the kitchen yowling.

"Hungry?" I asked the cat.

"*MROWR!*" she cried louder.

"I understand the feeling," I mumbled. "Let's look at the options."

Bugle continued to miaow while I checked the fridge and freezer. I found chicken nuggets, leftover lasagna and turkey slices. Nothing raw. Nothing good.

"I lose," I told the cat. "But there has to be something here for you."

I dug around in the cabinets for Bugle's food. I found the cans, plus an added bonus for me. In the back behind sunflower seeds and dried pasta was a bag of beef jerky.

I pulled it out and examined the label. *Do they cook beef jerky?* I wondered.

I ripped the bag open. It was worth a shot. I quickly shoved the strip of meat into my mouth.

Too quickly!

CHAPTER 4

"The cat has my tongue!" I shouted into my phone. Only it sounded more like, "Wuh wah wu mu munh!"

On the other end of the line, Jaybee had no idea what I was saying. "Tulah, is that you?" he asked.

"Uh-huh," I mumbled.

"Are you OK?" he asked.

"Unh-unh. Unh enh oo-oo um uhvah." Of course I wasn't OK. I couldn't speak. I needed Jaybee to come over and help me!

My brother sighed. "Are you still at the Gregors' house?"

"Uh-huh," I mumbled again.

"All right," Jaybee said. "I'm coming."

44

He ended the call. I peeked into the living room to check on Max and Libby. They had turned on the TV. The kids must have been so wrapped up in their programme that they hadn't heard me coughing. Staring mindlessly at the screen, they looked more like zombies than I did.

I hoped the programme would keep them busy for a bit longer. I couldn't let them know their cat was hiding somewhere with one of my vital parts in her paws!

Pacing back and forth, I waited for Jaybee. Then I realized I needed a way to explain what had happened. It's not like I'd just be able to tell him. (It's really hard to talk without a tongue.) So I grabbed a pen and a piece of paper and started writing.

When I had finished my note, I waited by the window. I opened the door before Jaybee could knock.

He looked grumpy. "What's wrong now—"

I quickly put a finger to my lips to keep him quiet and not interrupt the kids' programme. I led him to the kitchen and handed him my note.

"The cat has your tongue? Like your *actual* tongue?" Jaybee whispered after reading the first line. His face broke into a grin. I could tell he was trying to hold back a fit of laughter.

I didn't smile or laugh. It was not funny. Not to me.

"Sorry," Jaybee said when he saw the look on my face.

I tapped my wrist to remind him that time was ticking by. What if Bugle *ate* my tongue before we found her?

Jaybee finished reading my note, and I handed him my phone. I needed him to call Angela immediately. As soon as I got a hold of my tongue, I would need her help sewing it back in.

But first, we had to catch that cat.

47

I checked my phone. Angela was here! Talk about perfect timing.

While Jaybee kept an eye on the kids from the kitchen, I sneaked Angela in the back door. We crept to the bathroom and locked ourselves inside.

Angela inspected the damage. "Oh dear," was all she said.

She quickly got down to business. She selected a curved needle from her tools, reached into my mouth and started to sew. The sight in the mirror made me cringe, but I didn't feel a thing.

"How did you manage to cough your tongue out?" Angela asked, sounding kind of impressed as she added another stitch.

I shrugged. With my mouth propped open and my tongue half on, I couldn't exactly explain. I wasn't even sure myself. The only explanation was that I was a complete freak. And a complete wreck.

"Thanks," I said when she was done. It was a relief to be able to talk again. I stuck out my tongue and checked Angela's work. "They didn't cover tongue reattachment in my sewing tutorials. Whoa, you did a great job. I can't even see the stitches!"

"They're invisible stitches. They're under the skin," Angela said. She sounded proud. "You should watch surgery videos instead. I've been picking up lots of tips from them."

"Yeah, maybe," I said with a sigh. I briefly wondered if I'd ever have a normal hobby again.

I peeked my head out of the bathroom door. Jaybee was heating the hot dogs for the kids. He gave me the all clear sign. The TV was still blaring as I tiptoed with Angela to the back door.

"I don't know how to thank you," I told her.

"Just try not to lose any more parts?" Angela suggested. She got on her bike and waved goodbye.

By the time Mrs Gregor got home, Jaybee had managed to get the kids away from the TV and feed them dinner. I had managed to stay together and not have any hunger-fuelled outbursts.

"Oh! Hi, Jaybee!" Mrs Gregor said as she walked in. Max and Libby immediately swarmed her.

"I asked him to come and help," I explained. "I hope you don't mind."

"Of course not," Mrs Gregor said. "But I can't pay both of you. You two will have to work out how to split the money."

I took the cash, but on the walk home I handed the whole wad over to Jaybee.

His face lit up. "Really? You're giving me all of it?"

I nodded. "You earned it," I told him. "After everything you did, I should probably pay you more." Except I didn't have more money. I didn't have *any* money.

My money-making scheme had failed.

I had failed.

I couldn't even hold myself together long enough to handle a simple babysitting job! Plus, I still hadn't eaten.

"*Auuugrrrhh.*" I let out a noise somewhere between a growl and a moan. I felt worse than ever.

Jaybee shot me a look and took a step away. I could understand his reaction. I wasn't fit to be around normal living people.

When we got home, I went straight up to my room. I hid under the covers like I used to when I thought monsters might be lurking under my bed. I was old enough to know there wasn't anything on the floor beneath me. The lurking monster was right under my quilt.

The monster was me.

CHAPTER 5

Bella Gulosi, my least favourite person
in the world, stood at the chalkboard in
Mr Stein's room after school on Tuesday.
Bella held a piece of chalk and spoke in
that know-it-all voice that made me wish
my ears had popped off instead of my
tongue. (And that I hadn't bothered to put
them back on.)

"Does anyone else have a theme idea
for the dance?" Bella asked. "*Anyone?*"
She blew her breath out her nose. Clearly
Bella had elected herself president of the
dance committee.

I rolled my eyes. After three days with
no meat, there was nobody I wanted to bite

more than Bella, and I was pretty sure
she felt the same way about me. Ever
since I had beaten her in a spelling bee,
she'd made it her mission to make
me miserable.

Two dance ideas were already up on the
board. They were written in Bella's perfect
handwriting:

UNDER THE SEA
AROUND THE WORLD

"Really? No one?" Bella said, managing
to sound annoyed. She turned back to the
board and started writing. "OK, then. I'll
add my idea."

A NIGHT TO REMEMBER

"I already want to forget it," I whispered
to Nikki and Angela, who were sitting
beside me.

I wasn't sure what I was even doing here.
My parents had finally gone shopping and
I'd wolfed down four eggs for breakfast.
But it had only been enough to bring my

mood from terrible to meh. I still needed to solve my food problem. That was not going to happen sitting in a classroom discussing dance themes!

I looked across the room. Jeremy and his friends were huddled together. They hadn't spoken a word to us since we got to Mr Stein's room. They were probably talking about my vomiting problem and wishing they'd never asked me to join the committee.

"How about a Monster Mash?" Jeremy suddenly blurted. He glanced over at me, and I froze. For a second I thought he had worked out my secret!

Bella stared at Jeremy. "A *what?*"

"A Monster Mash dance. I think it'd be a good theme because the dance is so close to Halloween," Jeremy explained. "Everyone can dress as a mash-up of two monsters, like, uh, Franken-Ghost or Drac-Zilla."

"*Oooh,*" Angela said. She suddenly perked up.

"I like it," Nikki said as she started to nod. "I could be a Zom-Banshee!"

Bella's face pinched up like she'd just taken a bite out of a lemon. Jeremy's idea was obviously a better idea than hers, and she hated that.

Normally I would've loved to watch Bella get shown up. But unfortunately I also hated the Monster Mash idea. It was just too close to home. I was already a monster mash-up, and it wasn't fun at all.

"I don't know," I started to say. "Costumes are kind of . . ."

I trailed off when I saw Jeremy's face fall. He wanted me to like the idea. But costumes weren't fun if you had to dress up every day just to look normal.

Bella immediately picked up on my less-than-enthusiastic attitude. She smiled big and was suddenly all pumped up again. The only thing she liked as much as winning was watching me lose.

"OK, let's vote!" Bella chirped.

Every hand in the room shot up, except mine. A few kids cheered, and Jeremy and his crew did some high-fiving. My bad mood took a turn for the worse.

"Good! It's decided!" Bella clapped her hands together and grinned.

Nikki and Angela were smiling too. "Now we have to decide on our costumes," Angela said. "Got any ideas?"

"Are unicorns monsters?" Nikki asked.

Angela nodded, and Nikki crossed her arms. "*Hmm.* Well, then that's going to make my decision even harder! What about you, Tulah?"

I shrugged. I didn't want to tell my friends I'd already made a decision. It was easy – I wasn't going to go to the dance.

CHAPTER 6

"I know you're disappointed that Jeremy didn't ask you to the dance, but you *have* to go," Nikki said over the phone the next day.

I sighed and sank onto my bed. Nikki had spent every spare moment at school trying to convince me to change my mind. Now she was arguing after school too.

"It'll be fun!" Nikki insisted. "Angela and I are going to work on our costumes together on Saturday. You should come!"

"Like I said, I'll think about it," I told Nikki. "But I kind of have other problems to deal with."

The truth was I *had* been thinking about the dance since the meeting on Tuesday.

After four days with no money and no meat, I was sure I was sticking with my decision.

There was no way I was going. I didn't have a date. I was *already* a monster. And I needed to focus on my next meal. Why didn't anybody get that?

"But it's going to be so *fuuuuun!*" Nikki gushed. "Come on!"

"News flash, Nikki. Being a monster is not fun!" I snarled into the phone. (Wow, I *really* needed to focus on food.)

"OK, OK. Don't have a cow," Nikki said.

I let out a harsh laugh. "I *wish*. A cow would be great right now." If only Nikki knew how hungry I was. Even the leather on my shoes was starting to look delicious.

"I mean, sorry, I . . . You've just been so grumpy lately," Nikki said. "Maybe you need a break. You know, lighten up, let go and live a little. You'll regret it if you don't go to the dance. I just know it."

"I gotta go." I quickly ended the call
before I said something really mean. Then
I flopped back onto my bed.

I lay there and pressed my hands onto
either side of my head, trying to think.
My fingers balled into fists. Before I knew
what I was doing, I was yanking out huge
clumps of hair in frustration.

"*Noooo!*" I groaned when I saw all the
black curls in my fingers.

I rushed to the mirror and checked the
damage.

"Great," I mumbled. "Now I'm dead, grey,
starving, pickled . . . and partially bald!"

King trotted into my room and started to
whine. He didn't care what kind of mood I
was in or that I was missing patches of hair.
He just wanted a walk, and everyone else
was at Jaybee's football match.

I looked down into his brown puppy eyes.
He whimpered again.

"OK, OK," I said. It wasn't his fault I was
a monster. Then again, it wasn't my friend's

fault either. "Just give me a second to glue my hair back on."

After some quick superglue touch-ups, I clomped down the stairs. Then I took King's lead off the hook by the door and clipped it on. He was so excited that he wagged his whole back end as we made our way outside and along the street.

I couldn't help but smile. It's hard to be grouchy when your dog is happy. Plus it was kind of nice to be walking out in the fresh autumn air. As hangry and monstrous as I was, I felt my bad mood start to lift just a little.

I froze as I had a brain wave. I suddenly knew the perfect way to make meat money!

"King, that's it!" I shouted.

King Kong looked up from his sniffing for a full second and then reattached his nose to the telephone pole.

"Dog walking!" I said. "That's a job I can do! Dogs have to be walked *every* day! We're talking steady income!"

King looked at me again. His tail was wagging, mostly because I kept repeating his two favourite words, *walk* and *dog*.

"And dogs won't care if I'm in a bad mood, or if I'm hungry or out of joint. It's perfect!" I squealed.

I tugged King's lead back towards our house. I wanted to get home and start making flyers. The sooner I got some clients, the sooner I could eat.

And the sooner I ate, the sooner I might start feeling human again!

"Yes, Ms Lee. I can pick up Count before eleven. Thank you!" I hung up the phone and added another dog to my list.

By Saturday morning, I had landed four dog-walking clients. It was a good thing too. I *really* needed money and meat.

"What happened to all the eggs?" Mum yelled from the kitchen.

"Sorry, Mum!" I yelled back. "I, uh . . . dropped them."

"Again?" Mum said. I couldn't hear her heavy sigh, but I could feel it. I knew she was mumbling about how clumsy I'd become lately.

I walked carefully down to the front door with my list of dogs and addresses. I called King and clipped on his lead. "I'll be back in an hour or so!" I shouted towards the kitchen.

It was time to collect the pack . . . and make some cash.

GRRRRRRRRR!

And so did I!

Or maybe my hanger was finally coming in handy!

CHAPTER 7

Who knew dogs and zombies spoke the same language? I certainly didn't.

I looked down at the five dogs sitting at my feet. They were all staring up at me, patiently waiting for my next command. All it had taken was one growl, and I had earned their total respect!

"*Grrrrr,*" I growled again, but this time it was my stomach reminding me that we were on a mission.

"Let's go!" I called to the pups. I knew exactly what the next stop on our walk had to be. My well-behaved dogs trotted down the street.

"Stay!" I told my pack.

The dogs immediately stopped and sat down. I tied their leads around the bench outside the butcher's shop. Before I pushed the door open, I gave another tiny growl to remind them who was in charge.

I stepped inside and was overwhelmed by the smell of fresh meat. It was the most delicious scent EVER. I licked my lips and wiped the bit of drool that started leaking from my mouth. If I wasn't careful, I could end up with a slobber spot the size of a lake all down my shirt!

The bell over the door rang as it swung shut. A woman dressed in white came out from the back and up to the counter.

"Can I help you?" she asked.

I nodded excitedly. Could she ever!

Hungrily I stared at all the raw options. I squinted to keep my eyes from popping out cartoon style. It all looked so GOOD!

I fumbled with the dog-walking money in my pocket. Then I started pointing out cuts of beef.

The butcher weighed my hefty selections. "Having a barbecue?" she asked.

I nodded again. I was so hungry I couldn't even speak to thank her! I just handed over all the money I had collected so far.

Cradling the package in my arms, I hurried for the door. It had been so long since I'd eaten anything this good. All I could think about was getting the dogs, finding a private place and then sinking my teeth into a T-bone steak!

I was in such a rush that I didn't notice someone was trying to come in at the same time I was trying to get out. I shoved the swinging glass door – right into Jeremy!

My crush stumbled back. I stumbled forward. Jeremy grabbed me just in time to keep me from hitting the pavement. But I was so startled I jerked away like he was made of stinky cheese.

"What are you doing here?" I demanded.

I clutched the package of meat to my chest and hoped he wouldn't ask me the same thing. I couldn't tell Jeremy Romero that I was buying a mountain of beef so I could wolf it down raw to keep from turning into a raging maniac.

"Well?" I added. Hungry Tulah was not very polite.

Jeremy looked embarrassed, like he'd been caught doing something strange. Only nothing could be as strange as what I was doing.

"I, uh, I was following you," he said sheepishly. "I was in the park, and I saw you go by. I, um, wanted to ask you—"

"You were *following* me?" I blurted out. My mind instantly started replaying memories of my last half-hour. *Did he see me growl at the dogs? Did he see me getting excited about the meat on display? OMG, what exactly did he see?*

Jeremy stepped back, and I stepped closer to the dogs, who were beginning to whine. They probably smelled my meal. I know I did.

"I just . . ." Jeremy stopped himself and looked at the big, paper-wrapped package in my hands, and then at the five dogs tied to the bench. "What's all the meat for?"

"Is that what you wanted to ask me?" I demanded. It sounded rude. I swallowed hard. It was difficult to think straight, let alone be civil.

The last couple of days at school, I'd just tried not to talk because everything that came out of my mouth was either kind of mean or kind of dumb. It was like my heart and my brain just couldn't work right without meat.

Which I had . . . in my hands . . . and I needed to EAT. Like, now!

"Well, no," Jeremy started again. "I was actually looking for you at the dance committee meeting yesterday after school to—"

"I quit the committee," I said in a rush. That was rude again. I shoved the meat into my backpack, even though all I wanted was to tear open the paper and dive in. I had to get away from Jeremy before things got worse.

Jeremy looked confused. "Oh. Because I—"

"I gotta go!" I said, freeing the leads. Jeremy gave me a strange, sad look as the dogs began pulling me away. "It's my new job," I tried to explain. "I'm a dog walker now. Too busy for committees . . ."

Meat. Meat. Meat. The word echoed in my head. Jeremy didn't move except to raise one hand in a wave. I looked back twice. He was still standing there, completely confused.

Meat. Meat. Meat.

When I was sure Jeremy wasn't following me again, I yanked on the leads. I pulled the dogs into an alley.

Meat! Meat! Meat!

I dropped the leads. I tore open the package as fast as I could, like a kid at Christmas. I was so excited I was shaking!

MEAT! MEAT! MEAT!

As soon as my belly was full, I felt kind of sick. It wasn't the kind of sick when I ate normal food. I was just, well . . . disgusted with myself.

My new appetite was nasty.

I wiped my mouth with the back of my hand. It was covered in blood.

King Kong walked over and licked my cheek. I wasn't sure if it was to make me feel better or because I tasted like steak.

"What am I doing, King? What am I *going* to do?" I asked him.

King whimpered.

I stared at the extra raw red meat sitting on the butcher paper next to me. I had wanted the food so badly that I'd eaten it with my bare hands.

At the beginning of the school year, I wouldn't have even touched a slice of lunch meat. I was a vegetarian! I felt bad about beheading lettuce.

Now look at me. I was the hungriest, most flesh-eating carnivore ever.

Slowly I wrapped up my leftovers. I should've been happy. I'd finally got what I wanted – what I'd been after for days. But now all I wanted was to be normal.

"Oh, King," I said. "Am I really going to be a freak show for the rest of my life?"

King whimpered again as I dropped the leftovers into my backpack and stood up. Then I let the dogs tug me towards their homes.

After we dropped off the last dog, I still felt horrible. King jumped up so his paws were on my knee. He always sensed when I was sad.

I stopped and looked into his sweet brown eyes. They reminded me of another pair of sweet brown eyes – Jeremy's!

"Oh no!" I slapped a hand over my mouth. "Jeremy was following me because he was going to ask me to the dance, wasn't he?"

I had been so hungry and so angry at anything and everything keeping me from my meal. I'd brushed Jeremy off and acted weird and rude.

I pictured him again, standing in front of the butcher's shop. He was waving and had that sad, confused look on his face.

"*Uuuuuuungh*," I moaned out loud. "He must think I'm absolutely awful!"

CHAPTER 8

I stumbled through our front door.
I unclipped King's lead and let my
backpack full of meat fall to the floor.

THUMP.

I scowled at the bag. I had been so eager
to eat that I had bought way too much
meat. Now I was left with a load of leftovers
that needed to get into a fridge – preferably
one that was not ours. And I needed to find
a place soon.

I texted Angela. I hadn't been a
particularly great friend lately, but I was
definitely what my dad would call "a friend

in need", and I was hoping Angela would be my "friend indeed".

ME: *Can I come over? I have a new issue of ZOMBIE BOY Z.*

That was code. *Zombie Boy Z* was Jaybee's favourite comic. I'd learned a lot about the undead from reading it, though obviously not everything (like where to store six pounds of steak without anyone asking questions). When I told Angela I had a new issue of *Zombie Boy Z*, she knew the *real* issue I wanted to share was all mine.

ANGELA: *Come on over. Nikki's already here!*

I froze. I'd forgotten Nikki was going to Angela's today to work on their monster costumes. I'd been trying to put all things dance out of my head.

I didn't want to be there while my friends prepared for a dance I wasn't going to. But I needed to take care of the extra food. Angela was my best bet for finding a solution.

So I wrote a quick note for Mum letting her know I'd be at Angela's. (Mum was getting her hair done while Jaybee and Dad went to the cinema – a classic monster film, of course.) Then I grabbed my backpack full of meat and headed to the garage to get my bike.

Both tyres were flat. I grumbled as I pumped them up and went back for my helmet. Angela was good at patching me up, but there was no excuse for taking silly risks.

When I got to the Stone Family Funeral Home, I rang the front doorbell.

DOOOONNGG. DOOONNGGG.

"*Yeeeess?*" A mummified hand appeared around the edge of the door. Then a . . . scaly fin? I thought I should run (or walk very quickly) away because something was NOT RIGHT. But then I heard Nikki's unmistakable giggle.

My BFF threw the door open the rest of the way.

"Ta-da!" Nikki threw up her shimmery wrapped arms and did a shuffling spin so I could see the fancy fish tail made with plastic scales and lots of glitter. "I'm a Mer-Mummy!" she exclaimed.

"Doesn't she look great?" Angela asked.

She was standing behind Nikki in the shadows. When she stepped closer, I saw she was partially in costume too. She'd glued bolts onto her neck and stitched tattered, patchwork wings onto a long, black suit jacket. I cringed when I saw she had fake stitches on her face – like the real stitches I tried to hide.

"We're making our costumes for the dance. I'm a Franken-Fairy!" Angela said. She spun around so I could admire her. "We would've waited for you, but we didn't think you were coming."

I forced myself to smile. The meat in my backpack suddenly felt ten times heavier.

Actually, all of me felt ten times heavier. Nikki and Angela stood there in the doorway, grinning and waiting for me to tell them how awesome they looked. But all I could think about was how awful I felt.

"You guys look great," I finally told them.

They really did too. It was just that they had been having fun dressing up like monsters. Meanwhile I was out walking dogs and doing everything I could to keep my monster identity a secret.

It just wasn't fair. What they did for giggles, I dealt with in the waking nightmare that was my life. Or my death. WHATEVER!

I wished I hadn't come. I wished I could cry. I couldn't make tears anymore, but if I could, they would have been flowing like a river.

My thoughts must have shown on my face, even without the waterworks. Because Nikki and Angela stopped smiling.

"Is something wrong, Tulah?" Nikki asked. "You don't look so hot."

"Maybe you should come in. You said you had a new issue?" Angela said.

She reached for my elbow to guide me into the house. I jerked away.

"You guys just don't get it!" I snapped. "This is all a joke to you." Even as I said the words, I knew I was being mean and unfair – and it wasn't because I was hangry. "Of course I've got a new issue. I *always* have a new issue!"

Everything was so easy for my friends but so weird and complicated for me.

"Maybe you need something to eat?" Angela suggested, backing away.

Nikki just stood there blinking.

"I just *ate*," I moaned. "That's part of the problem."

I let my backpack drop to the ground. I felt the anger drain out of me, replaced by complete hopelessness.

"I can't even deal with my *leftovers*!" I sobbed, but without tears. "I can't do anything right. I have to spend all my time trying to have a semi-normal life, and I still feel like a total monster!"

Even though I'd just gone off at her, Nikki stepped closer. She put her arm around my slumped shoulders. "You're not a *monster* monster," she said. "You're Tulah Jones!"

Nikki pulled me inside. Angela picked up my bag from the porch and closed the door.

"Yeah, do monsters sing in musicals?" Angela asked. "Do monsters save their best friends from falling stage lights?"

"No," I admitted.

"Don't think for a second you're some mindless zombie," Nikki said, wrapping me in a tight hug. "You're our best friend, and you're funny and totally fantastic."

I squeezed back. "I guess I'm not *just* a monster. . . ."

Angela peeked inside my bag and lifted an eyebrow. "Nope. You're a monster carrying around a *lot* of meat," she added.

I couldn't help it. I smiled. "Right? That's my issue."

"That's not an issue. That's so great!" Nikki said. She clapped her hands together. "That's just what you needed, isn't it? How'd you get the money to buy all of it?"

"I started walking dogs today, and I made enough to go to the butcher's shop," I explained. "I think I can make dog walking a regular job. But now I have to find a place to put all my steaks."

"That's perfect!" Nikki shouted. She was so happy she started bouncing on the balls of her feet. Her mermaid tail fluttered up and down.

Angela nodded. I could tell by the lines on her forehead she was already starting to think of solutions.

"Was dog walking fun? It sounds fun!" Nikki asked while the wheels in Angela's head kept turning.

"Yeah, I guess," I had to admit. "It was pretty fun. Until I saw Jeremy."

"Oh!" Nikki put a hand over her mouth and stopped fluttering.

Angela started pushing us towards the kitchen. "OK, T," she said. "Why don't you give us the lowdown while I start chopping. I know just what to do with your leftovers."

"Really? What?" I asked.

Angela took off her Franken-Fairy outfit and hung the jacket on a chair. Then she went to the kitchen worktop, got a knife and unwrapped my meat.

"My parents just got a new freeze-dryer," Angela explained. "It preserves flesh. It'll be able to dry the beef without any cooking. So technically it'll still be raw. The best part is, once it's dried you won't have to keep it cold. It won't go bad."

"No way!" I exclaimed. Now it was my turn to bounce and flutter. It sounded too good to be true. "Angela, you're amazing! This could actually be a long-term solution to my hanger problem."

"So what about the other problem?" Nikki asked while Angela sliced and diced the meat. "What happened with Jeremy?"

I sighed and leaned against the worktop. "I think he was going to ask me to the dance. But I had a hangry outburst and totally freaked him out. I'm pretty sure I ruined any chance with him."

"Oh no, that's rough," Nikki admitted. "But you know, you don't need Jeremy to ask you to the dance. You can come with us and still have a fantastic time. You really should."

I stared at the floor. "But . . . it feels like the Monster Mash will be making fun of freaks like me," I told her.

"First of all, you are *not* a freak. And second, everyone will be too busy *having* fun to make fun of anyone!" Nikki said, striking a pose in her Mer-Mummy get-up.

Angela stepped back from the worktop with a tray full of meat strips. "Nikki is right, Tulah. Besides, being normal is overrated. Let me put these in the dryer. Then, I have something else I think you might like. . ."

We went into Angela's room.

You've already got the zombie look.

All you need is the mash.

Here. Try it on!

Count Zomb-Ula! You look amazing!

I twirled, and the cape swung out. It went all the way to the ground and made me look like I was gliding as I walked. I could not stop looking at my reflection in the full-length mirror.

"Wow," I said. I spun left and right, letting the cape flow around me.

All I needed were fangs and some blood for the Dracula part. Then I could just take off a bit of my corpse make-up so I'd look my own zombie shade of grey.

"It's perfect!" Nikki gushed.

"Yeah," I nodded. "It really is."

I was no horror fan like Jaybee, but even I had to admit it was a pretty fabulous look. Dressing up *was* fun, and so was letting a little of my zombiness shine! I felt better in my undead skin than I had in a long time. Never underestimate a good pep talk from your besties.

"OK," I said. "I'm definitely going to the dance."

Even though it was disappointing not to be going with Jeremy, going with my two friends could be just as good. Maybe even better!

Nikki jumped up and down and squealed. Angela grinned.

I gave one more twirl in the mirror, thinking about how great the dance could be. For once, I would not be the odd one out!

CHAPTER 9

"Look out!" a voice yelled.

I ducked in time to avoid a ball of gauzy fabric flying past my head. It was the next Friday after school, and we were draping the fabric all over the multi-purpose room to make it look creepy for the dance.

"Sorry!" Nikki panted as she trotted over. She flashed me a grin.

"No problem," I said, brushing off the near miss. I tacked up another piece of fabric over the door.

The dance committee had let me join in the decorating even though I had stopped going to meetings. I had to admit, I was having fun.

Angela and I had painted a fake lake (with an Elf-Ness monster swimming in it) before she had to go home. Then Nikki and I had worked on creating a cemetery in the corner by the cupcake table. In another corner, a group of kids made a swampy forest complete with a three-headed Bigfoot stomping around.

The room was basically monster paradise! It looked like we were going to be ready just in time for the dance later that evening.

"We need more tombstones for the front!" somebody walking in called.

It was Jeremy!

I quickly ducked behind the ladder I was using and kept my face to the wall. I'd been successfully dodging Jeremy all week. I hadn't said a word to him since my rotten rudeness during the dog-walking incident.

Which reminded me, I had to get home soon. I needed to walk the dogs before the dance!

I pulled out my phone and checked the time. "Nikki, what time is your mum picking us up?" I asked in a whisper.

Nikki checked her own phone. "She should be here in about fifteen minutes. Do you want to come over and get ready with me?"

I shook my head. "Sorry, I can't. I need to walk the dogs first, then get a bite to eat and then get dressed. I'll have to meet you here," I explained.

I stood back to admire our work, feeling proud. A week of food had done me a world of good. Now that I had a steady job, I had a steady supply of beef. And thanks to Angela's amazing freeze-dried meat jerky (which was a bit chewy but totally tasty), I could save it up without it going bad.

I might be a freak, but I was *not* freaking out today. Even though time was tight and I was a little hungry, I was keeping it together.

I rushed out of the room before Jeremy could say another word. I had a schedule to keep if I wanted to get to the dance on time. And apologizing to Jeremy for my major freak-out? That could take a million years!

"Ta-da!" I said as I swirled into the living room at home.

My vampire cape was ON, and the make-up that kept me from looking like a zombie was OFF. Not wearing lots of make-up felt amazing. I was finally just *me* . . . with a cape and fangs.

"Sweetie, you look fantastic – I mean *terrible*!" Mum said, clapping her hands.

"It's kind of cool," Jaybee admitted.

Dad covered his neck with one hand and the top of his head with the other. "I don't know which to protect, my blood or my brains!"

I laughed and gnashed my fake fangs at him. "Don't worry. All I need is a lift."

Dad grabbed his keys, Mum blew me a kiss and Jaybee crossed his fingers for me. Ten minutes later I was making my way through tombstones to the entrance of the Monster Mash Dance!

The fog machine was pumping out clouds, and the lights were down low. I squinted into the dark, looking for Nikki or Angela.

Bump!

Somebody ran into me, and I turned on them. "Watch it, Squid-Squatch!" I snapped at a kid with a furry head and tentacles.

The kid rushed away, and I suddenly realized I never grabbed a snack after school. I hadn't eaten since this morning, and I was already starting to feel the effects. If I didn't dial it down and get something to eat, my costume was going to get a little too realistic!

I felt a tap on my shoulder.

"Hey, T!" Angela said, sneaking up behind me. She was already eating a cupcake decorated like a ghost.

"Hi, Angela," I said, staring as she took another nibble of her cupcake. I didn't want nasty baked goods, but the sight of gnawing teeth made me jealous.

Angela noticed my laser-like focus on her food. "That reminds me," she said. "I knew you wouldn't be able to have any of the snacks here. So I brought one for you. It's beef fresh from the freeze dryer."

She pulled out a bag from inside her Franken-Fairy jacket. I grabbed it and immediately tore into my protein treat.

"Thanks, you're a death-saver!" I told Angela between bites. As I chewed on the dry flesh, I could feel my hanger disappear.

Nikki arrived just as Angela and I finished our goodies. She let out a happy scream and said, "Your look is to *die* for, Tulah! Come on. You have to show it off!"

She dragged Angela and me out onto the dance floor.

"Nikki, you know I can't really dance anymore," I started to argue.

When we were working on the school musical, I had nearly torn off a limb trying to bust a move. I was such a terrible dancer that the choreographer, Ms Raimi, mostly had other kids dance around me.

"What are you worrying about? This will be perfect," Nikki said with a wink.

She held her hands up like a zombie. Then she lurched from side to side with the beat.

That's right! I thought, looking around at all the crazy costumes. I was surrounded by monsters. I didn't have to worry about looking like a zombie or dancing like a freak, because *everyone* was! This was a night to enjoy!

"OK, ghoul-friends, let's do this!" I said, flashing my fangs at Nikki and Angela.

We joined in the fun. I let my body move the way it wanted to the music. Soon a circle had formed around us. Other kids started copying my zombie moves!

"Go, Tulah!" I heard a familiar voice call.

I looked over towards the cupcake table to see Jeremy. He was dressed like a werewolf from the Black Lagoon: fifty per cent hairy beast, fifty per cent slimy sea creature, one hundred per cent adorable.

He smiled at me. I smiled back without thinking, then quickly spun around so my back was to him. I started to panic.

"Is Jeremy still looking over at me?" I asked Nikki.

She peeked over my shoulder. "Yep."

"Does he look . . . mad?" I asked.

"Nope," Nikki said, bobbing her head in time to the music.

"He just looks like somebody who wants to dance," Angela said.

"Yeah, somebody who wants to dance with *you*," Nikki added. She tugged on Angela's jacket sleeve, and they started grooving away.

"What?" I jerked my head up and whirled back around.

Suddenly I had two left feet. Two DEAD left feet.

I was crashing into everyone. At the last second I saved myself from splatting on the floor. . . .

BONK!

Ah!

"Your costume is perfect," Jeremy said. "You even have special effects to go with it!" Jeremy shook his head like he couldn't believe what had just happened. TBH, I couldn't believe it either. If my heart wasn't already snoozing in my chest, popping an eyeball definitely would've stopped it!

But in a way, I guess I *was* cool. Or at least keeping cool. I'd just stuck my eye right back in, no problem. I was getting a handle on this zombie business, and everyone else thought it was part of my act!

Jeremy danced closer, still looking at me like I was a double rainbow. "If there was a prize for best costume, you'd win for sure. How'd you do that eye thing?" he asked.

"You *don't* want to know," I said with a smile. "A vampire never tells her secrets."

"Of course not!" Jeremy laughed, then looked around shyly. "Seriously, Tulah. I . . . I think you're really awesome. I'm sorry for forcing you into joining the dance committee and for following you the other day. I know

I'm awkward. When we were in the musical, I always knew what to say. My lines were written down. But without a script, I get nervous and . . ."

Jeremy took a deep breath as he bounced on his toes. "The thing is, I like you. And I miss rehearsing. I want to hang out. So I was trying to work up the courage to ask you to the dance." He paused and let out his breath. "You must think I'm a freak."

I must think he's *a freak?* I thought. I had to bite back a laugh. Jeremy was hardly a freak, and I should know. I would've never guessed *he* was worried about talking to *me*.

Which made me think. If a guy like Jeremy felt weird and awkward . . . maybe *everybody* did. Maybe I wasn't so different after all. Maybe we all felt like mashed-up monsters sometimes.

Jeremy cleared his throat. "So, will you?"

I looked into his eyes. "Will I what?"

Jeremy smiled and asked, "Will you go to the dance with me?"

CHAPTER 10

The music changed, and the fog machine kicked into overdrive. I could hear Angela and Nikki calling to me from the dance floor. Without stopping to think, I grabbed Jeremy's hand and pulled him to the centre of the room.

"Yes," I said, leaning so close to Jeremy his wolf whiskers touched my grey zombie cheek. "I'll go to the dance with you."

We grinned at each other so hard I had to look away so I wouldn't split my face.

Nikki and Angela danced over to us with Noah and Charlie. Noah was dressed like some sort of weird bat thing and Charlie was a Goblin-Corn, with a single horn stuck on his head. Nikki's and Angela's costumes were the best, though. Nikki's mermaid scales shimmered in the pulsing lights, and her mummy wraps waved. Angela's wings flapped, and somehow she made stitches look glamorous.

When the song changed, my besties and I all shrieked.

"'Thriller' is the best!" Jeremy shouted. "Do you know the dance?"

Did I ever!

"Yes! Nikki!" I screamed for my friend. I turned back to Jeremy. "Nikki taught it to me. She learned the whole thing for a Halloween flash mob."

Nikki danced over with Angela right behind her.

Of course I had never performed it or danced it with anyone other than Nikki. Before I died, I was too nervous to do anything in front of a crowd. But I'd practised it in my bedroom and dreamed about a million times of dancing it with a group of people.

Tonight was the night.

Jeremy smiled wider and held up his claws. "Awesome! Then let's show everyone how it's done!"

With Nikki and Angela behind me and Jeremy by my side, I lurched left. I lurched right. I spun around and cocked my head to the side, like my neck was broken. I slid and shimmied and staggered and spun.

Soon, all around me other kids were also reeling and stomping and dragging their limbs. I don't know if we looked as cool as the dancers in Michael Jackson's video, but I felt cooler.

The creepy laugh at the end of the song echoed through the room, and I realized I was laughing too. I felt fantastic – better than I had in a long time. I was surrounded by friends who liked me, whether I was a monster or not. It suddenly didn't matter one bit that I was dead.

Words that every kid (living and dead) should know – brought to you by me, your friendly neighbourhood zombie!

TULAH'S TERMS

appetite desire to eat and drink stuff. My appetite for quality protein is on overdrive lately!

cannibal (this is really gross, so prepare yourself) a person who eats other humans. Zombies in stories often eat people, but I could never, EVER do this.

carnivore animal, or zombie, that only eats animal flesh . . . yum

civilized acting with good manners and being respectful, just like your parents taught you

committee group of people who meet and decide things, like what the school-dance theme should be

corpse simply put, a dead body

craving wanting something in the worst way. Please, never let me crave human brains!

embalming fluids special liquids used to stop dead things from rotting. Formaldehyde is one kind. If a living person drank this stuff, it'd kill them. Good thing I'm already dead.

flesh soft parts of a person or animal . . . like the parts I want to eat

formaldehyde gas that when dissolved in water makes the perfect mixture to stop almost anything dead from rotting. It's really helpful for smelly zombies!

funeral home place where dead people are prepared for burial or cremation. Also the place where I can get all patched up.

income money that you make from working. My dog-walking business is the perfect way to get an income. Now I can buy meat whenever I need it!

lurch move with a jerky motion, and how zombies walk. I'm not going to win a dance contest anytime soon.

protein thing found in foods like meat, dairy, eggs and beans that everyone needs in their diet. But zombies can ONLY eat protein, and it has to be raw animal protein like meat or eggs.

repulse cause you to feel so grossed out you have to get away from it

tutorial something that gives you detailed, broken-down information on a specific subject. It could be a small class, a book or (my favourite) a video.

vegetarian person who doesn't eat meat. Hard to believe my raw-meat-loving self was ever satisfied with just vegetables, fruits, grains, nuts, eggs and dairy.

USE YOUR BRAAAAINS!

Don't worry, I won't eat them.

SHPLAAAT!
FLUSSHHH!

I barely escaped to the toilets before The Blob escaped from my stomach.

1. Ugh. It's almost too embarrassing to even think about, but what is happening behind this door? What's making the SHPLAAAT and FLUSSHHH sounds? (Check page 28 if you need help.)

2. I wonder . . . what did Jeremy think about my hangry rudeness? Go back to Chapter 7, and try telling the butcher's shop scene from my crush's point of view. Talk about it with a friend. Or if you're feeling creative, write it like a story!

3. You can't see details as I cough out my tongue. It's all in silhouette (which is a fancy word for a dark outline against a lighter background). Why do you think this moment is shown like this?

When it finally came loose, something else flew out with it . . .

4. I was feeling super stressed. Being a zombie is tough! But even when I was alive, I could get freaked out. Share your advice. Write a list of five things kids could do when they're stressed.

5. OMG. My eyeball is dangling from my head! I was so surprised I can hardly remember what happened. How did my eye pop out? And more importantly, why isn't everyone freaking out? (Flip back to pages 98-100 if you need to refresh your memory.)

But maybe I was still doomed!

6. Raw meat is delicious (for a zombie). And yet . . . when I finally got my hands on some steak, I felt pretty grossed out and sad after I ate it. Help me out. Explain in your own words why I was feeling down after visiting the butcher's shop, even though I had a full stomach.

OMG, ZOMBIE!

After eating a suspicious school meal, I feel different. REALLY different. Find out how my undead life began!

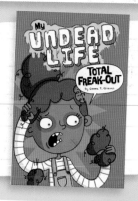

REALLY ROTTEN DRAMA

I'm dealing with a BFF crisis, my first-ever (stage) kiss and my rotting zombie body! Can I put an end to this stinky situation?

TOTAL FREAK-OUT

No meat equals one grumpy zombie. Can I get enough food to keep my mood under control before the school dance?

GOT BRAINS?

I'm going on a retreat with the academic team (and my nemesis, Bella Gulosi!). Will I survive the weekend?

About the Author

Emma T. Graves has written more than ninety books for children and has written about characters both living and dead. When she's not writing, Emma enjoys watching classic horror films, taking long walks in the nearby cemetery and storing up food in her cellar. She is prepared for the zombie apocalypse.

About the Illustrator

Binny Boo, otherwise known as Ellie O'Shea, is a coffee addict, avid snowboarder, puppy fanatic – and an illustrator. Her love for art started at a young age. She spent her childhood drawing, watching cartoons, creating stories and eating too many sweets for her own good. She graduated from Plymouth University in 2015 with a degree in illustration. She now lives in Worcester and feels so lucky that she gets to spend her days doing what she adores.